# HOTEL ANIMAL

Story
and
Pictures
by

KEITH DUQUETTE

VIKING

To my wife, Virginia

VIKING
Published by the Penguin Group
Penguin Books USA Inc., 375 Hudson Street, New York, New York 10014, U.S.A.
Penguin Books Ltd, 27 Wrights Lane, London W8 5TZ, England
Penguin Books Australia Ltd, Ringwood, Victoria, Australia
Penguin Books Canada Ltd, 10 Alcorn Avenue, Toronto, Ontario, Canada M4V 3B2
Penguin Books (N.Z.) Ltd, 182-190 Wairau Road, Auckland 10, New Zealand

Penguin Books Ltd, Registered Offices: Harmondsworth, Middlesex, England

First published in 1994 by Viking, a division of Penguin Books USA Inc.

1   3   5   7   9   10   8   6   4   2

Library of Congress Cataloging-in-Publication Data
Du Quette, Keith. Hotel Animal / by Keith Du Quette.  p.   cm.
Summary: Dismayed by the size of Hotel Animal and its guests, a
tiny lizard couple struggles to find small pleasures in a big world.
I S B N  0 - 6 7 0 - 8 5 0 5 6 - X
[1. Lizards—Fiction   2. Animals—Fiction.   3. Size—Fiction.
4. Hotels, motels, etc.—Fiction.]   I. Title.
PZ7.D9285Ho   1994   [E]—dc20      93-14531   CIP   AC

Printed in China
Set in Madison

Camille and Leon Lizardo owned the local insect market. They worked long and tiring hours selling bugs and flies to their fellow reptiles. They could barely keep up the pace.

So they decided it was time for a vacation. They took two suitcases from the closet and carefully packed them with their finest clothes. Then they closed up their market and set out on the great open road. They were so happy. Vacation, vacation, fun and games, rest and relaxation!

They drove and drove and finally came to a sign
for the Hotel Animal, the favorite vacation spot
for animals from around the world.

When they arrived, Camille and Leon were surprised. The Hotel Animal was big. Bigger than any building they had ever seen. They had to strain their little necks to see the top. Their hearts raced with excitement as they pushed with all their might on the heavy front door.

The hotel lobby was abuzz with activity. All sorts of large guests were relaxing and enjoying their vacations. Camille and Leon stood in awe. They felt very small and out of place, but this was the Hotel Animal, and they remembered they were animals just like the other guests. They held hands and bravely made their way to the front desk.

At the front desk they were warmly greeted
by Tomas, the hotel owner. He gave the
tiny couple a room key and rang
the bell for the old bellhop.

After a long climb up the stairs,
they had to climb even higher just
to put the key into the door.

Their room was very nice to look at, but much too big. They unpacked their bags on the thick shag rug. Then they put on their bathing suits and went down to the pool for a swim. They were really beginning to relax.

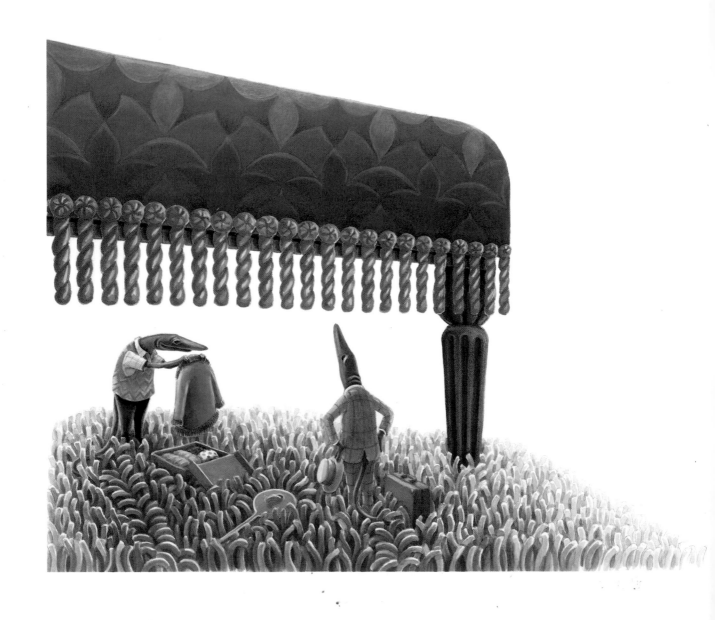

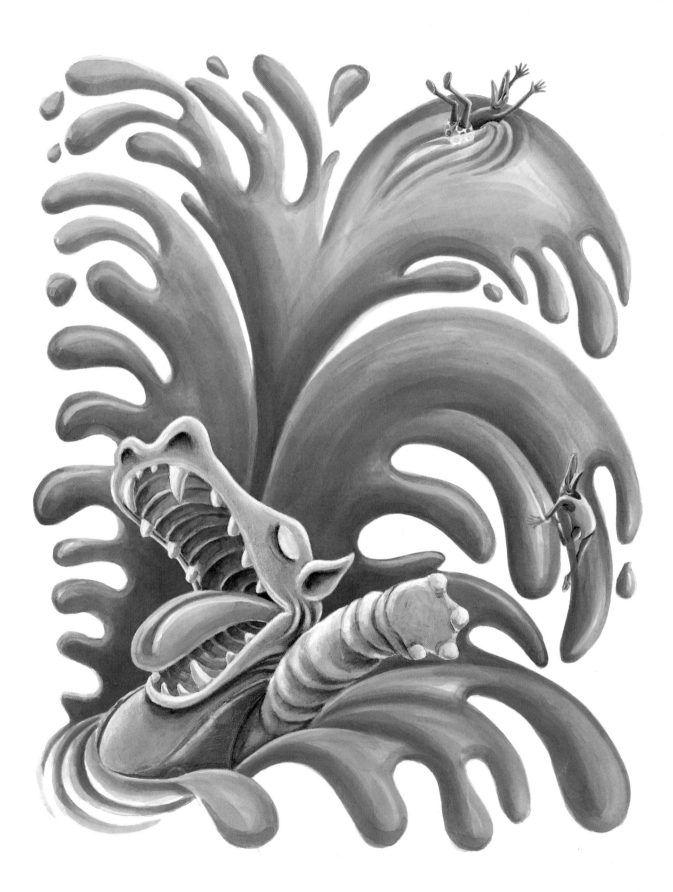

Suddenly, an enormous hippo jumped into the water with a great splash and sent Camille and Leon flying. The little couple landed with a thud on top of a sunbathing guest. They peeled themselves off the sunbather and said they were very sorry.

All of this activity left Camille and Leon feeling hungry. They went down to the hotel restaurant for some nice food, but it was not nice at all. Not only were there no insects listed on the menu, the food was too difficult to eat. To make matters worse, the other diners were shocked by the lizards' table manners.

This vacation was turning out to be no fun at all. Everything was too big, too high, too far, too heavy. This vacation was even harder than work.

Camille and Leon wanted to have a good time.
They gave it one last try. That night they put on
their finest clothes and went to a party in the hotel
ballroom. The Leo Scat Orchestra played great,
swinging songs. Camille and Leon did their favorite
dance, the jitterbug. Finally they were having fun.

But all of a sudden the dance floor was crowded
with excited guests who danced rumbas and
waltzes, mambos and tangos, and separated little
Camille from tiny Leon.

Then a ribbon from a balloon tangled around Camille's waist and lifted her off the floor. She yelled "LEEEONN" as loud as she could, but no one heard. She rose higher and higher above the dancing crowd. Everyone looked so small, but Leon was by far the smallest.

Up and up Camille went until
she heard a loud *pop!* The balloon
had burst on a crystal chandelier.
Way above the dance floor,
Camille held on for dear life.
There was nowhere to go but up,
so she pulled herself with all
of her strength through
a tiny hole in the ceiling.

Camille sat all alone in the hotel attic. She might
have been very little, but her fear was very big.
After a while her eyes adjusted to the darkness.
She got up and bravely explored the musty attic.
It was crowded with old and unusual things.

To her surprise she found a house. It was beautiful.
If only the Hotel Animal were like this, she thought.
She knew that Leon would love it, too, but he was
not there. She cried herself to sleep in a bed that fit
her just right.

Meanwhile, back downstairs, the music had
stopped. Everyone pitched in to find the missing
guest named Camille. They looked in all the places
a little animal might be found, but she was nowhere
to be seen.

Tomas, the hotel owner, felt terrible. He would
not rest until she was found. He put sad Leon
on his shoulder and searched every inch of the
Hotel Animal, from the basement on up. They
searched all night.

By the next morning, she still had not been found.
There was one final place to look. It was a place
that even Tomas, big Tomas, was frightened of.
They went through a trapdoor into the attic. The
creaking noises of the old attic floor woke Camille
from her sleep. She hid under the covers. Then she
heard a tiny voice call *"Camille!"*

It was Leon! They were together again. Tomas watched the happy couple in the little dollhouse. He remembered this old dollhouse and how much fun he had had playing with it when he was a cub.

"Wouldn't it be the perfect place for a vacation?" Camille said to Leon.

This gave Tomas a great idea. He lifted the dollhouse from the attic floor and carefully carried it down to the hotel lobby. He found a little piece of wood and painted a sign that read HOTEL ANIMAL TOO.

Now, whether big or small, all the animals of the world can have a grand vacation by checking into the Hotel Animal . . . or the Hotel Animal Too!

The perfect place for little
Camille and Leon Lizardo.